George Brown, CLASS CLOWN

Hey! Who Stole the Toilet?

**For Amanda, who for some reason really likes camping—with or
without indoor plumbing—NK**

For Maria—Mum away from Mom—AB

visit us at www.abdopublishing.com

Reinforced library bound edition published in 2014 by Spotlight, a division of the ABDO
Group, PO Box 398166, Minneapolis, MN 55439. Spotlight produces high-quality reinforced
library bound editions for schools and libraries. Published by agreement with Grosset &
Dunlap, a division of Penguin Young Readers Group.

Printed in the United States of America, North Mankato, Minnesota.
102013
012014

 This book contains at least 10% recycled materials.

Library of Congress Cataloging-in-Publication Data

This title was previously cataloged with the following information:

Krulik, Nancy E.
  Hey! who stole the toilet? / by Nancy Krulik ; illustrated by Aaron Blecha.
  p. cm. -- (George Brown, Class Clown)
  Summary: George cannot wait to go on his first camping trip with the Beaver Scouts, but
once in the wilderness his magical super burp returns, awakening animals including, perhaps,
the Ferocious Furry Frog.
  [1. Behavior--Fiction. 2. Camping--Fiction. 3. Scouting (Youth activity)--Fiction. 4. Magic-
-Fiction.] I. Title. II Series.
  PZ7.K9416 Hf 2012
  [Fic]--dc23   2011031483

ISBN 978-1-61479-218-5 (Reinforced Library Bound Edition)

George Brown, CLASS CLOWN

Hey! Who Stole the Toilet?

EXPLORER

by Nancy Krulik

illustrated by Aaron Blecha

Grosset & Dunlap

An Imprint of Penguin Group (USA) Inc.

Chapter 1

"Tzee. Tzee. Tzooooo!"

It was Sunday morning. The Beaver Scouts had gathered at Beaver Brook Park for their weekly meeting. But nobody was paying attention to the troop leader. Instead, the scouts were shooting one another funny looks. Why was George Brown **squeaking and squawking**?

"Tzee. Tzee. Tzooooo!" George squawked again.

"Cut it out!" Louie covered his ears. "Is that what you call singing?"

Louie's two best friends, Max and Mike, both started to laugh.

TZOOO!

"I'm not singing," George told Louie.

"Tell me about it," Louie said. "It sounds like two cats fighting."

"Yeah, cats," Mike agreed.

"In a big fight," Max said. "With **claws and everything**."

"I happen to be *calling*," George explained.

"Yeah right," Louie said. "How do you call someone without a phone?"

"Like this," George told him. *"Tzee. Tzee. Tzooooo!"*

The Beaver Scout troop leader, Mr. Buttonwood, ducked down as two yellow, brown, and white birds flew overhead.

"Tzee. Tzee. Tzooooo!" the birds called back to George.

"Okay, George," Troop Leader Buttonwood said with a laugh. "Enough with the birdcalls!"

"You really sounded like a bird!" Alex, George's best friend, told him.

"Yep," George said proudly. "It's the call of the warbler. And it's the sound we're going to hear coming out of my birdhouse when I hang it under  that tree over there." George held up a rectangular box made of wood. It had a hole in the front. He had built the birdhouse to earn his **Carpentry badge**. "I brought the kind of seed warblers like to eat, too."

"How do you know what warblers like to eat?" Louie asked him. "Do you speak warbler?"

"He was just talking warbler," Max told Louie. "Don't you remember?"

"Yeah. *Tzee. Tzee. Tzooooo*," Mike added.

Louie scowled. Mike stopped **tzee-tzee-tzooing**.

"I know about things like birdseed because I work at Mr. Furstman's pet shop," George told Louie.

Louie didn't answer. Instead, he showed the scouts **a huge birdhouse**. Actually it looked like a bird apartment building. **It had four floors and sixteen little tiny rooms.**

"Wow," George blurted out. He couldn't help it.

"No way he made that," Chris whispered to Alex and George. "He must have bought it."

"I made this all by myself," Louie told the other boys.

"Well, with the help of my big brother, Sam," he added.

4

"More like with the help of the guy his dad paid to help Sam help Louie," George whispered. Alex and Chris laughed.

"This is a house for purple marlins," Louie continued. "I'm going to put it on my front lawn."

"You don't want to hang it here in the park and share it with everyone else in our town?" Troop Leader Buttonwood asked.

"No," Louie said.

"He's being **selfish**," Chris said.

"Nah, he's just being Louie," George said.

"It's a really cool birdhouse." Max complimented Louie.

"Yeah," Mike agreed. "You should get **an extra badge** for having the best one."

"This isn't a competition, boys," Troop Leader Buttonwood told them. "Scouting is about being the best person you can be."

"I'm definitely the best," Louie said. "Just like Sam. When he was in the Beaver

Scouts he had so many badges he had to get **a second sash**. Sam got almost every badge there is. The only one he's missing is **the Explorer badge**."

"And you boys are all going to earn a lot of badges during our camping trip next weekend," Troop Leader Buttonwood told the boys. "The campground is right near the Bahka Wahka Ocka River, so you'll have a chance to earn your Canoeing badges. And we're going to earn Hiking badges, too. And, of course, you will get your Cooking badges after we make meals over an open fire."

"We're going to have so much fun," George said excitedly. He'd never been on an overnight campout before.

"Yes, but this trip is going to be hard work, too. Camping separates the men from the boys!" Troop Leader Buttonwood reminded everyone.

George looked around. The only boy he wanted to be separated from **was Louie**.

"The first rule of camping is to be prepared. Here's what you need to bring." Troop Leader Buttonwood started to pull a pile of papers out of his backpack.

"Whoops!" Troop Leader Buttonwood shouted as **a big wind came and blew** the papers out of his hand. "The packing lists!"

The troop leader took off trying to catch the lists. But as soon as he grabbed one paper, another blew farther away. Then his scout leader's hat blew off his head and **landed in a tree**.

Troop Leader Buttonwood reached up to grab his hat. *Bam*. He slammed his head into a low-lying branch.

"I'm okay," Troop Leader Buttonwood told the boys as he **rubbed a lump** growing on his forehead. "I *meant* to do that—to show you how important it is to watch out for low-lying branches when we're in the woods."

"I guess he wasn't prepared for that wind," George said.

"Well, *I'm* prepared to earn **a lot of badges**," Louie said. He looked over at George and laughed. "It's too bad they don't give out a badge for **acting goofy**," he said. "You'd get that one for sure."

George looked down at the ground. He didn't even answer Louie. What could he say? It was the truth. George did act goofy—a lot. But it wasn't his fault. **Not at all.**

It was all the fault of a **stupid magic super burp**.

It all started when George and his family first moved to Beaver Brook. George's dad was in the army, so the family moved around a lot. George had plenty of experience at being the new kid in school. So he'd expected the first day in his new school to stink. First days always did. But *this* first day was the stinkiest.

In his old school, George had been the class clown. He was always pulling pranks and making jokes. But George had promised himself that things were going to be **different** at Edith B. Sugarman Elementary School. **No more pranks.** No more squishing red Jell-O between his teeth and telling everyone it was blood. No more imitating teachers behind their backs. **No more trouble.**

Unfortunately, being the well-behaved kid in a new school also meant that George was the new kid with no new friends. No one at Edith B. Sugarman Elementary School even seemed to know he was alive—except for Louie, who seemed to hate him from the minute they met.

After that terrible, rotten first day, George's parents took him out to Ernie's Ice Cream Emporium to cheer him up. While they were sitting outside and George was finishing his root beer float, **a shooting star flashed across the sky**. So George made a wish.

I want to make kids laugh— but not get into trouble.

Unfortunately, the star was gone before George could finish the wish. So only half came true—**the first half**.

A minute later, George had a funny feeling in his belly. It was like there were hundreds of tiny bubbles bouncing around in there. The bubbles hopped up and down and all around. They ping-ponged their way into his chest and bing-bonged their way up into his throat. And then . . .

George let out a big burp. A *huge* burp. A SUPER burp!

The super burp was loud, and it was *magic*.

Suddenly George's arms and legs started going crazy. It was like he had lost control of them. His hands grabbed straws and stuck them up his nose like a walrus. His feet jumped up on the table and started dancing **the hokey pokey**. Everyone at Ernie's started laughing. The laughing sounded great—**just like the old days**. Unfortunately, his parents yelling at him *also* sounded a whole lot like the old days.

The magical super burps came back lots of times after that. And even though Alex was trying really hard to help George **squelch those belches once and for all**, so far Alex hadn't been

able to find a cure. And so the burps just kept on bubbling, and the trouble just kept on coming.

Like the time the magical super burp made George start dancing *up* the down escalator at Mabel's Department Store. Or the day it made him skateboard **right into a bucket of papier-mâché goo** in the art room. Or the time the burp made him bounce so

high on a
trampoline
that **his tighty
whities** got caught on
a tree branch on the way
down. Ouch. **Talk about the
world's worst wedgie!**

George was really worried about
what might happen if the magical super
burp followed him into the woods for
the campout. The idea of the super
burp going wild *in* the wild was just too
frightening to think about.

Chapter 2

"Okay, soldier. Now that we've got the tent set up, **it's time for mess**."

George grinned. He knew what mess meant. It meant food. And George was pretty hungry. He had asked his dad if they could have a practice campout. That way George would be prepared for the real one with the Beaver Scouts.

"Come on, soldier," George's dad said. "Let's get these burgers on the grill."

As George's dad starting grilling, George split apart buns, topping each side with a slice of cheese. **It was fun camping with his dad**—even if it was only in the backyard.

Suddenly the walkie-talkie in George's pocket **started to buzz**. Actually, it was only his mom's cell phone. But for today, George and his dad were calling it a walkie-talkie. George looked at the caller ID. It was his mom calling George from inside the house.

"Hi," his mom said. "I just looked out the window and saw that it was getting windy. Do you want me to bring out your jacket?"

"No, Mom," George said. "I'm fine."

"How about your slippers?" his mom suggested. "Your feet may get cold."

"You don't bring slippers on a camping trip, even if it's just in the backyard." **George took a deep breath.** "I gotta go, Ma," he said finally.

"Okay," his mom said. "But you can call later if you need something. Or if you decide you'd rather sleep inside."

"Soldier, it's time to pour the **bug juice**," George's dad said as George hung up the phone.

"Roger that," George answered. He poured **two big glasses of bug juice** and sat down. The juice was bright red—it looked like it was made of **spider blood**. Except it wasn't really. It was actually just sugar and water and red food coloring.

"See? Isn't living in the great outdoors wonderful?" George's dad said as he brought over a pile of burgers.

"Definitely," George agreed. He took a big bite of burger. A **glob of ketchup** shot out from under the bun and landed on his sweatshirt. George just left it there. He didn't have to clean it. Soldiers didn't call dinnertime *mess* for nothing!

"I think tonight we soldiers better be on the lookout," George's dad told him.

"For what?" George asked. "Enemy soldiers?"

George's dad shook his head. "No. For your *mom*." He took a bite of his burger, and **a giant glob of mustard** shot out and landed on his pants. "She's liable to come out here and make us use napkins!"

"Did you and your dad have fun last night?" Alex asked the next afternoon as the boys took a table at the Pizza Palace.

"Yeah," George said. "We had a great time. **Real messy!**"

Just then Mr. Tarantella, the guy who ran the Pizza Palace, walked over to their table. "Hey, guys," he said. "So? What'll it be?"

George looked at the menu. Ordering pizza was serious business. You had to pick just the right toppings. "Um . . . I think today I'll have a personal-size pizza with

sausage, pepperonis, and meatballs."

"I'll just have a plain, personal-size pizza," Alex said.

"You got it," Mr. Tarantella told them. "Coming right up."

"So now you must be really psyched about the scout camping trip," Alex said.

"I guess," George said. But he didn't sound so sure. "I've got all my gear ready. I just hope **something else** doesn't sneak along with me."

"You mean sneak *out* of you," Alex said. Alex was the only other person in the whole world who knew about **the magic super burp**. George hadn't told another soul. He figured people would think he was nuts.

Actually, George hadn't *told* Alex about the burp, either. Alex was just so smart that he'd figured it out. "Maybe if I find a cure, it'll be like a medical breakthrough! I'll be in the news. Who knows. **I could win a Nobel Prize.**"

"Alex, I don't think a whole lot of people are suffering from—from you know whats." George pointed to his belly. "I'm probably the only person on the planet."

Alex nodded. "True. Well, even if I don't get famous, I still want to find a cure for you . . . last night I read about a new way to get rid of gas," Alex told George.

"It doesn't sound that hard. All you—"

"Shh . . . ," George warned. He pointed toward the door. Louie, Max, and Mike had just walked into the Pizza Palace.

"All you have to do is chew each bite of food a hundred times before you swallow," Alex said, lowering his voice to a whisper. "The food will just **slide down**. You won't swallow any air with your food. It's swallowing air that makes you burp."

Hmmm. Chewing wasn't hard to do. It was worth a try, anyway.

"I'll have a personal pie with extra cheese and anchovies," George heard Louie say.

Ugh. Now George didn't feel like he had to burp. He felt like he had to *puke*. Who would order pizza with **hairy fish all over it**?

Louie, that's who. And Max and Mike, too, of course. They copied everything Louie did.

"Hey, guys." Julianna waved to George and Alex. She was with Sage.

George was kind of surprised to see Julianna with Sage. Julianna was more like one of the guys. And Sage was . . . well . . . **she was just weird**.

"Did you order already?" Julianna asked them.

Sage gave George **a huge smile**. "Hi, Georgie."

Grr. George hated when Sage called him that. So he looked away and watched Carlo, the guy behind the counter. It was so cool. First Carlo would take a ball of dough and start rolling it and stretching it out. Then he'd toss the pizza dough up in the air, catch it, and toss it again, turning it into a flat circle. Sometimes

Carlo would **spin around on his heels** and then reach up and catch the dough. Sometimes he would close his eyes. But he never missed. **Not once.** It was amazing.

Sage tapped George on the shoulder. "I like your skeleton T-shirt," she said, looking at George's black-and-white T-shirt. "It's so macho!"

"We're . . . uh . . . kind of in the middle of something," George told the girls. "Beaver Scout talk."

"We're planning for our campout next weekend," Alex explained.

"I love camping," Julianna said. "My family has been taking me camping since I was a baby."

"Being surrounded by nature is so beautiful," Sage added. "Don't you think so, **Georgie**?"

Georgie . . . er . . . *George* groaned. "It's not a beautiful kind of trip," he explained. "It's a **mud-sliding, mosquito-biting, no-showering kind of trip**."

"Not to mention scary stories," Louie added from his seat across the room.

"Wait until you hear the one about the monster that lives by the Bahka Wahka Ocka River. Sam told me that one a long time ago."

"Yeah right." Julianna rolled her eyes. "I'm not scared of **monsters**."

"Of course not," Louie told her. "Everyone knows there's **no such thing as monsters**."

For once, George had to agree with Louie. **No one in fourth grade** believed in monsters anymore.

A moment later, Mr. Tarantella came by with two pizzas. Yum!

"I wish we could come on the trip," Julianna said.

What? Did Julianna mean Sage and her? George was taking his first bite of pizza and practically choked.

"Well, no way is that gonna happen. This trip is just for Beaver Scouts," Louie told Julianna. "You're not a scout. **Tough luck.**"

"Sage and I used to be **Nature Girl Scouts**," Julianna told the boys. "But then our troop leader moved. Doesn't that count?"

"No," Louie told her.

Julianna looked mad. Sage looked sad. Without another word they walked off and took a booth in the far corner of the restaurant.

"Now don't forget," Alex said as he watched George eat, "you gotta chew each bite a hundred times."

George nodded. He opened his mouth and took another bite. Then he started to chew. And chew. **And chew some more.**

The pizza turned into a mushy glob of tomato, cheese, sausage, pepperoni, and meatball goo in his mouth.

Chew. Chew. Pizza grease and pepperoni juice slipped out the sides of his mouth.

Chew. Chew. Red sauce ran out of George's mouth **like blood**. Little slimy bits of sausage came sliding out and landed on George's T-shirt. He was a mess, but it was for a good cause!

And then, suddenly, George felt **something brewing** in the bottom of his

belly. Something bing-bongy. And ping-pongy. The super burp was back. And all the chewing in the world wasn't keeping it down.

"Dude, not again," Alex said nervously.

Yes, again. But before George could even nod, **his mouth burst open**. Gooey, chewy pizza slime drooled all over him. And then . . .

Mamma mia! That was one loud burp!

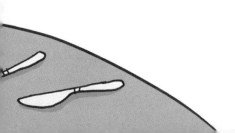

Chapter 3

George opened his mouth to say, "Excuse me." **But that's not what came out.** Instead, George's mouth shouted, "Time to make some pizza!"

Before George knew what was happening, his legs started running across the restaurant behind the counter where Carlo tossed the dough.

"George, no running in the restaurant," Mr. Tarantella said as he brought out more pies for customers.

"Watch out! George is acting goofy again," Louie said. "That kid is **so weird**."

"The weirdest," Max agreed.

"The goofy weirdest," Mike added.

George jumped onto the counter. His hands reached down and picked up **a big blob of white, squishy dough**.

"Hey, you can't do that!" Carlo yelled at George.

"No? Just watch me!" Then George started throwing the dough up in the air and catching it. Soon the dough began to spread into a circle. He tossed the pie-shaped dough over and over, **higher and higher**.

"Dude, come on. You have to stop," Alex called.

But George didn't stop. He couldn't. He wasn't in charge anymore. It was like he was one of those old-fashioned puppets and someone else was pulling the strings.

"Woo-hoo!" George's mouth shouted out. "Who wants a piece a pizza?"

George's hands reached up to catch the flying dough on its way down and . . . **missed**! The big blob of dough landed right on George's head and oozed down over his face. **George poked two holes out for his eyes.**

"George Brown, stop it right now!" Mr. Tarantella shouted at him.

"I knew it. I knew he'd **freak out**!" Louie kept shouting.

Suddenly, George felt something go **pop in his belly**. It was like someone had just stuck a needle in a balloon. All the air rushed right out of him.

The super burp was gone. Everyone was staring at him like he was out of his mind. Then he opened his mouth to say, "I'm sorry." And that was exactly what came out.

"I can't believe Mr. Tarantella threw us all out," Louie groaned. "I didn't even do anything. It's **all your fault**, George." Louie started up the street. Then he turned back. "I'm warning you. You better not pull anything goofy on our camping trip. I don't want to be sent home early from that, too."

George gulped. Was there any chance at all that **the super burp would stay away for a whole weekend**? Somehow, he doubted it.

"I'm sorry you didn't get to eat your pizza. I owe you, dude," George said to Alex as they walked home.

"It wasn't a total waste. I got two pieces of chewed gum from under the table," Alex said. Alex was trying to break the *Schminess Book of World Records* for the largest ABC gum ball.

George wished he could be happy for Alex. But he was too upset about what had just happened. He was **so embarrassed**, he didn't think he could ever show his face at the Pizza Palace again. Grr . . . first the burp had made him freak out at Ernie's and now the Pizza Palace. If this kept happening, George wouldn't be able to go into any restaurants in Beaver Brook. **He'd probably starve to death.**

"I thought you were doing a really good job tossing that pizza dough," Sage told George. "At least until it landed on your head."

"It was pretty funny. You looked like a

ghost made out of dough," Julianna said.

"Thanks." Then George mumbled under his breath to Alex, "The chewing didn't work."

"It's okay, dude. I'm working on it," Alex whispered to him. "I'll come up with something."

"Boy, George, you just can't stop getting in trouble," Julianna said. "I wish I were going on the camping trip—just to see what kind of trouble you get into."

George groaned. There was **nothing funny** about the super burp—at least not to him.

Chapter 4

"A Beaver Scout is honest and true.
A Beaver Scout knows what to do.
A Beaver Scout is a loyal friend.
He'll be your friend right to the end.
A scout is strong, and a scout is tough.
We are Beaver Scouts, and that's enough."

George said the Beaver Scout oath along with his pals at the troop meeting on Wednesday night. He was really excited. **This was an important meeting.** They were there to discuss Saturday's big camping trip!

"Okay, scouts." Troop Leader Buttonwood sat in the middle of a big circle in a room at the community center.

"I have big news. **Two new scouts are joining our troop.** They'll be here any minute! I know you're going to give them all a big Beaver Scout welcome."

"Who are they?" George asked.

The door to the room **burst open**.

"I'm sorry, are we late?"

Julianna and Sage were dressed in Beaver Scout uniforms and carrying Beaver Scout guidebooks.

"Hi, guys," Julianna said to the scouts.

"Hi," Sage added. "Did I surprise you, Georgie?"

George was so surprised, he **couldn't answer**.

"You don't belong here," Louie said. "We're having our Beaver Scout troop meeting."

"We're Beaver Scouts," Julianna told him. "See? We have the uniforms and the guidebooks."

"Yeah, we bought them yesterday," Sage added.

"Girls can't be Beaver Scouts," Louie told Julianna and Sage.

"Who says?" Julianna asked him.

"It's in the guidebook," Louie told them.

"Wrong!" Julianna held up her guidebook.

"Actually, the girls are right. The new guidebook was changed. Now a Beaver Scout doesn't have to be a boy," Troop Leader Buttonwood told everyone. "It just says a Beaver Scout has to be between the ages of eight and eleven and work to earn badges. **Welcome to Troop 307, girls!**"

43

Louie was so mad, it looked like **steam was going to come out of his ears**. "This is so wrong!" he shouted. "My dad is going to be **really mad** when he hears about it. He's gonna sue. And he can, because he's a lawyer. He'll take this case all the way up to **the Supreme Court** if he has to."

"Well, until he does, the girls are part of our troop," Troop Leader Buttonwood told Louie. "And we will treat them with respect like any other scouts."

Julianna and Sage smiled and sat down in the circle. Julianna tried to sit next to George, but Sage **squeezed in between them**.

"Isn't this great, Georgie?" Sage asked George. She **batted her eyelashes** at him. "We're going to spend the whole weekend together on a camping trip."

George didn't answer. He had really been looking forward to the camping trip. Now, between the super burp and Sage, **so much could go wrong**.

Beaver Scouts were supposed to be prepared. So George spent the next few days preparing for the campout in his own way. He did everything he could think of to put **an end to the magic burps**. He didn't drink any soda. He didn't eat beans. He chewed each mouthful of food he ate one hundred times. He figured that maybe Alex's "cure" needed longer to work. It took forever to get through a meal, and his jaws **ached like crazy**. Still, he hadn't burped once in three days. That was a good sign, wasn't it?

Or was the burp hiding, waiting to pop out on the camping trip?

"You're sure you have everything?" George's mom asked as she said good-bye to George at the campgrounds on Saturday morning.

"Yep, I'm good," George said. "Dad helped me pack last night."

"You have an extra sweatshirt in case it gets chilly at night?" his mom asked.

"Yep. And my toothbrush," George said. "I told you that in the car."

"Okay," his mom said. "I'm going to leave then. Have a great weekend."

As his mom drove off, George lugged his gear over to where Alex and Chris were.

"Cool stuff," Chris said. "Is it all **genuine army**?"

"Yep," George said proudly. He looked down at his dad's old camouflage-print sleeping bag and his **regulation US Army** water canteen. Having a dad in the army was **pretty cool** sometimes.

"I got my sleeping bag from my aunt for my birthday last year," Chris said. Chris's sleeping bag had comic superheroes all over it.

"Mine's just a regular sleeping bag," Alex said. "But the guy at the store said it would keep me warm. And I brought my binoculars, too."

Just then, Louie drove up in a limo. He got out, carrying his guitar—and that was it. **He didn't have any gear at all.** *Weird.* A minute later, Max and Mike arrived. From the back of a van, they got out lots and *lots* of gear.

You practically couldn't even see them underneath **the pile of sleeping bags, battery-operated fans, plastic folding lawn chairs, a blow-up mattress, and big cans of bug spray**.

"Louie! Hey, Louie!" Mike shouted. "We brought everything you said. No worries!"

Just then, George felt someone clap their hands over his eyes.

"Guess who?" a voice behind him asked.

George might not have been able to see anything, but he could hear just fine. "It's you, Sage," he grumbled.

"Yes," Sage said, taking her hands away from George's face. "I'm here and ready to go camping."

George **kicked at the ground** and frowned.

"Hey, guys," Julianna said, walking up the hill just behind Sage. "Ready to go?" Julianna's backpack was **really cool**. It was covered with patches from **all over the world**.

"France, Spain, Argentina, Egypt, Israel, South Africa, Nigeria." George read the names of the countries on the patches. "Hey, how do you say this one?" he asked, pointing to the patch that read KYRGYZSTAN.

"I don't know," Julianna answered. "My parents brought it back from a trip." She fingered the compass she was wearing on a rope around her neck. "They brought this back from the rain forest in Costa Rica."

"Did you see **my new boots**, Georgie?" Sage asked.

Sage was wearing **bright pink rubber boots**.

"Why are you wearing rain boots?" he asked her. "It's not supposed to rain."

Sage shrugged. "Julianna told me I needed boots."

"*Hiking* boots," Julianna said. "Not rain boots."

"But these were prettier," Sage said. "Hiking boots only come in black or brown. And these pink boots match my necklace and my bracelet."

George rolled his eyes. What kind of Beaver Scout wore pink boots and jewelry? A *Sage* kind of Beaver Scout.

Just then, Troop Leader Buttonwood started to run over to where the scouts were standing. *Bam!* A minute later he was on the ground. He'd **tripped over one of the laces** on his hiking boots.

"I'm okay. I'm okay," he told the scouts. "I *meant* to do that. Just wanted you all to make sure you tied your bootlaces."

"I don't have laces," Sage said. "Rain boots don't have laces." She

turned to George. "But your boots do. Better double knot **the bunny ears** so you don't get hurt, Georgie."

Louie and his Echoes started to laugh. George wondered if there was **a badge for being annoying** on a camping trip—because it sure seemed like Sage was doing her best to earn it!

Chapter 5

Thump!
Bump!
Plop!

"Oh no, not again," George groaned as his tent **fell down on top of him** . . . again. He crawled out from under the thick, green tent tarp and looked up at Alex and Chris. "Why can't we get this thing to stay up?"

"That last time it should have worked," Alex said. "It shouldn't have collapsed, at least not according to **any rule of science**."

"I don't think science has anything to do with this," Chris said.

"Sure it does," Alex said.

"It's physics because . . ."

George had already stopped listening to Alex, right around the time he said *science*. It was good to have a really smart friend. But right now, Alex's science smarts **weren't helping at all**.

"We have to try it again," George said. He picked up the tent poles and started putting them back together.

George and his buddies weren't the only ones having a tough time with their tent. Louie, Max, and Mike were struggling, too. Well, Max and Mike were, anyhow. Louie was busy sitting on a folding chair, strumming his guitar.

"Oomph," Max groaned as he **jabbed himself with a pole**.

Louie's tent was huge. It had **big flaps that went up and down** on the sides and windows with netting to keep out mosquitoes.

"Hurry up," Louie said to Max and Mike. "I want to be first to get our tent all set up."

"Sorry," Mike apologized. "We'll try and work faster."

Max looked down at the instructions that came with Louie's tent. "These aren't in English," he said. "Anyone here speak Japanese?"

"There," Julianna **announced suddenly**. "All finished."

George looked over to where Julianna and Sage were standing. Sure enough, their tent was set up.

"You guys need any help?" Julianna asked, walking over to where George, Chris, and Alex were struggling.

"Yeah," George said. "I can't get the poles to stay together."

"That's because you've got them **upside down**," Julianna said. "Here, let me show you." She picked up the poles and fit them together. Then she grabbed the tarp. In about five minutes, the boys' tent **was standing tall**.

"Aaaahhhh!" Suddenly Louie jumped out of his chair and started screaming. "Bug! Bug! Get that thing away from me!" He picked up two cans of bug spray and started **spraying wildly in the air**.

"CUT THAT OUT!" Sage shouted. Everyone stopped and stared. Sage did

a lot of goofy things. But she didn't
usually shout. "Bugs are living things,"
she told Louie. **"You can't just kill them!"**

"Oh no?" Louie asked her. "Watch
me." He sprayed at the air again.

"What did that bug ever do to you?"
Sage asked Louie.

"He bugged me," Louie said.

Max and Mike began to laugh.

"The bug bugged him," Max said. **"Get
it?"**

"Good one, Louie," Mike added.

"Bug spray isn't good for the
environment," Julianna told Louie. "I've

got something better." She reached into her backpack and pulled out a candle.

"A candle?" Louie asked. "What's a candle gonna do?"

"It's a *citronella* candle," Julianna corrected Louie. "It has a smell that keeps mosquitoes and bugs away without killing them."

"Great idea, Julianna," Troop Leader Buttonwood told her. "You came prepared like a good Beaver Scout should. And because you did, you have earned the first badge of the camping trip—**the Ecology badge**. Congratulations!"

Sage gave Julianna a hug. "The bugs all thank you," she said.

Louie just rolled his eyes. Then he turned to Max and Mike. They looked really proud because they had finally gotten the tent to stand.

"You guys set the tent up with a rock

right in the middle!" Louie yelled at them. "I'm not sleeping on any rock."

But then Max said, "That's okay, I'll sleep on the rocky part. It won't hurt me. My dad's always saying I've got **rocks for brains**, anyway."

George laughed. That was actually pretty funny—even if old **rocks for brains** Max didn't get the joke.

Troop Leader Buttonwood asked for everyone's attention. "Okay, before we go on our canoe trip, there are a few safety rules I want to go over with you," he said.

"First, we need to keep the campsite clean, and we need to keep all the food locked up in the crates I brought along."

"That will keep the raccoons away," Julianna said.

"Exactly," Troop Leader Buttonwood agreed. "There are **all kinds of animals** in the woods. Most of them won't bother us if we don't bother them. Except, of course, if we happen to **run into Triple F**."

"Who's that?" George asked.

"That's the dumb monster all the troop leaders tell stupid, scary stories about." Louie looked at Troop Leader Buttonwood. "Right?"

"Maybe the stories are stupid . . . and **maybe they're not**," Troop Leader Buttonwood said.

"Well, you've never *seen* a monster, have you?" Louie insisted.

Troop Leader Buttonwood shook his

head. "But just because I haven't seen one, doesn't mean they don't exist."

George shivered a little. He didn't believe in monsters. But what the troop leader had said made sense.

Troop Leader Buttonwood turned to all the scouts. "Enough about the rules. Let's head down to the river, put on our life jackets, and go canoeing!"

"Yay!" the kids all cheered excitedly.

As the scouts headed down to where the canoes were docked, Alex whispered to George, **"How's the gas situation?"**

George shrugged. "So far, so good."

"I hope it stays that way," Alex told him. Then he held up **two crossed fingers**.

Chapter 6

"I don't see why we can't have three people in a canoe," George grumbled as he put on his yellow life jacket. "It's not fair."

"Sorry, dude," Alex said. "If we want our badges, we have to do it with two people in a canoe. Don't be mad at us. Troop Leader Buttonwood's the one who put you in a canoe with Sage."

"It won't be so bad," Chris said. "You don't have to talk to her."

This really stunk. Chris and Alex got to be together in a canoe. Max was with Louie, and Mike was with Julianna. But George was stuck in a canoe with Sage. **This was the worst!**

"At least you're not with Louie," Alex pointed out.

That was true. Being with Louie **would be worse**.

"Come on, *Georgie*," Sage called to him. "Let's get paddling."

Or maybe not. **Being with Sage was going to be awful.**

"I'll go in front," Sage said as George climbed into the canoe. "You can be in the stern and steer because you're stronger than me."

George climbed into the back of the canoe. **This trip wasn't turning out the way he'd hoped.**

But a few minutes later, George felt happier. He was paddling down the river. And he realized he didn't have to pay attention to Sage. He could just focus on steering the canoe around the bends in the river. Every now and then Sage lost control of her paddle and **splashed herself**. That was pretty funny.

Suddenly, a strong wind started to blow. The canoe picked up speed.

"Wahooooo!" George shouted. "This is awesome."

"Yikes!" Sage cried. "Georgie, we're going too fast. Make it stop!"

"How?" George asked.

The canoe **bounced up and down**. And then George noticed *something else* bouncing around. GAS! And it was bouncing in his belly.

Oh no! The **super burp was back**—right in the middle of the Bahka Wahka Ocka River. George wasn't sure what the burp might do if it escaped now. All he knew was it would be *ba-a-ad*!

George had to stop that burp! He started rocking back and forth. Maybe he could put the burp to sleep.

"Georgie, stop that! We'll tip!" Sage shouted.

The burp kept bouncing. **Bing-bong! Ping-pong!**

George twisted to the left. He twisted to the right. Maybe he could twist his stomach into a knot and tie off the burp. He . . . *splash!* **The canoe tipped over!**

"Aaaaaah!" Sage cried out as she fell into the river.

"Whoops!" George shouted as he went under.

Pop! Just then, George felt something burst in his belly. All the air rushed out of him. George had **squelched the belch**!

"Yahoo!" he shouted.

Oops. George was still underwater. The minute he opened his mouth to let out that *yahoo,* he let *in* a whole lot of cold river water—**and a wiggly, jiggly fish, too**!

But that was okay. Nothing mattered except that George had **beaten the burp**! His head popped up out of the water and he gave a big "V for Victory" sign.

"Georgie! Georgie! Help!" Sage cried out suddenly.

George looked over at Sage. She was bobbing in the water. And the canoe was moving down the river.

"Help me!" she cried again.

George knew Sage really didn't need help. She was wearing a life jacket. And the water was only a few feet deep.

"Georgie, I'm a bad swimmer," Sage cried out again.

Beaver Scouts had to be prepared. So George guessed he better be prepared to save Sage before saving the canoe. He started to swim to her. **But the current was strong.**

Suddenly, Sage started swimming to George. When she reached him, she **wrapped her arms around his neck**. "Oh, Georgie! Pull me to shore."

A minute later they were both standing in the mud on the side of the river.

"I thought you said you were a bad swimmer," George grumbled as he struggled out of Sage's arms.

"Um . . . well . . . I am. Usually," Sage said. "I guess it was just your *animal magnetism*. It drew me right to you. **You saved me.** I was going under. I could see my life flashing before my eyes. I was in a tunnel with light at—"

George didn't wait to hear any more. He jumped back in the water and swam to the canoe, which had gotten stuck onshore a little farther down the river. George flipped it back over. Now it was right side up and **ready to go**.

Troop Leader Buttonwood canoed over to them. So did the other kids.

"Are you okay?" the troop leader asked Sage and George.

"He saved my life," Sage said. "Georgie is a hero."

Louie laughed. "More like a *zero*. Did you guys see how he flipped that canoe over?"

Max and Mike cracked up. But Troop Leader Buttonwood didn't laugh at all. "Did you see how George flipped it back? That's exactly what you're supposed to do **when a canoe capsizes**. George also knew to come to the aid of another scout first. So George is getting **two badges**. One for canoeing and a special one for water safety."

"Wow," Alex said. "Two badges. Impressive, dude."

"Thanks," George said. "It was no big deal."

"That's not fair!" Louie shouted. "If I'd known I could get another badge, I would have **flipped my canoe**."

"Yeah," Max said. "And he would have flipped it better. **Louie's always flipping.**"

"Exactly," Mike agreed. "No one flips out like Louie."

"Now that we know everyone's okay," Troop Leader Buttonwood said, "let's get paddling back to camp." He was about to step into his canoe when he **lost his balance.**

Whoosh! Troop Leader Buttonwood went sliding. He landed face-first in **slimy mud**.

"It's okay," he called back to the kids. "I *meant* to do that. I was just trying to show you how much fun it is to go mud-sliding."

"That looks like fun," Julianna said. She slid down the mud, too.

"Awesome!" George exclaimed. He lay on his back and swished down in the mud feetfirst.

"Check it out!" Chris shouted. "It's Toiletman to the rescue!" He got **on his belly** and **slid face-first** down the muddy hill and into the river.

"Hey, George!" Alex cried out. "Think fast!"

George grinned as Alex threw **a huge pile of slimy, grimy, gooey mud** right at him. There was mud in his hair, in his ears, and under his arms. Some mud had even slimed its way into his bathing suit and **onto his butt**.

This was really fun. Normal kid fun. Not the super burp's idea of fun.

BONK!

Chapter 7

"Hey, watch out!" Louie shouted at George. "You **almost hit me** with that tree branch."

George moved out of Louie's way and carried his pile of wood down to the fire pit. His arms were really tired. He'd carried a lot of wood to the campsite. So had everybody else. Well, everybody but Louie. He pointed out which pieces of wood Max and Mike had to carry for him.

"Whoa!" Max shouted as he banged into a tree. He couldn't see over the **humongous pile of branches** he was carrying.

"Hey, check out **these paw prints**," Chris called out suddenly. "They're huge."

Alex, George, and Sage stopped and stared down at the ground.

"You don't think they're **bear prints**, do you?" George asked his friends.

Alex shook his head. "Bear prints have four round toes. These prints are long and skinny. And way bigger. Besides, the Beaver Scouts would never let us go camping here if there were bears in the woods."

"Then what kind of tracks are they?" George asked him.

"I think I may have an idea," Troop Leader Buttonwood said **mysteriously**. "I'll tell you all about it tonight."

"He's going to tell us they belong to a monster, just like Sam said he would," Louie joked. "Like anyone would believe that."

"I wouldn't believe it," Max said.

"Me neither," Mike agreed.

For once, George thought Louie and the Echoes were right. **There were no such things as monsters.** Still, the tracks were right there. And no one seemed to know what kind of animal they could belong to.

"At least the tracks are heading away from the campsite," Sage pointed out.

That was true. The tracks were heading **straight into the woods**.

"*We* better make tracks!" George said. "The sooner we get this wood to the fire, the sooner we eat!"

A little while later, Julianna was busy at the fire pit helping Troop Leader Buttonwood build the fire.

"Hand me some more twigs," Julianna told Chris. "We have to finish building this pyramid so we can start the fire."

"Georgie and I collected a whole lot of twigs," Sage told Julianna. "He's got a great eye for twigs."

George kicked at the dirt. **Sage hadn't left his side all afternoon.** How was he ever going to get rid of her?

When the wood was all laid out, their troop leader **lit a match**. "Ouch!" Troop Leader Buttonwood shouted suddenly. He wiggled his finger in the air.

"Are you okay?" Julianna asked.

"Um . . . yeah," he said as he blew on his finger. "I *meant* to burn my finger. I wanted to teach you kids to be careful with matches. Fire safety is a big part of camping."

"It takes teamwork to build a fire," Troop Leader Buttonwood continued as he handed out sticks for cooking hot dogs. "That's why you're all getting your **Fire Safety badges**."

That didn't seem very fair. Louie hadn't done anything. But George didn't say that. It would be tattling. **And George Brown was no tattler.**

Rumble. Grumble.

Just then, George felt something rumbling in the bottom of his belly. *Rumble! Grumble! Gulp!* Oh no! Was the burp back?

George's stomach rumbled again. It grumbled again. And then it didn't do anything else. **George was just hungry!**

Soon George was holding a long stick over the fire. He watched his hot dog plump up.

"I love hot dogs," Alex said as he moved his hot dog over the fire next to George's.

"Me too," George said. "Especially when they're burned a little." He pulled his stick out of the fire and plopped the hot dog on a bun. A minute later he took a big bite. "Oh yeah! Perfect!" he said and then began chewing **a hundred times**, just to be on the safe side.

"We have marshmallows, too," Sage said later, once everyone had finished off two hot dogs. She smiled at George. "Would you like me to make you **a toasted marshmallow**?"

"No thanks," he told her. "Cooking 'em is half the fun." He stuck three marshmallows on his stick and went back to the fire.

Max and Mike were already roasting marshmallows. "Done!" Max said. Then he ran over to Louie. "I made a marshmallow for you."

Mike was right behind him. "No way! *I* was making one for Louie."

"I made mine first," Max said.

"I made mine better," Mike insisted. He shoved a cooked marshmallow in Louie's face. "Try it."

Max tried to shove Mike's stick away.

"Ow!" Louie shouted suddenly. **A goopy marshmallow was stuck right on his nose.** "Who did that?"

"It was him," Max and Mike said, pointing at each other.

George started to laugh. Louie was standing there with a toasted marshmallow

hanging off the tip of his nose like **a ginormous, white booger**!

Camping sure was great!

Once the sun had gone down, the woods grew very dark. Besides the campfire, the only light came from the full moon. George was glad that they'd collected so much wood. If that fire went out, it would be **really spooky out there**.

"I know I told you guys about the raccoons and the bats," Troop Leader Buttonwood said suddenly. "But I think you should also be on the lookout for the **Ferocious Furry Frog**."

"The what?" George asked.

"Here it comes!" Louie said. "The monster story. What did I tell you?"

"The Ferocious Furry Frog," Troop Leader Buttonwood repeated. "Or **Triple F** as some call him. He's part frog and part bear. **And he's huge**."

Troop Leader Buttonwood stroked his chin. "I've never seen him myself," he went on. "But they say he lives in these parts. And he doesn't like company."

"Is this for real?" Chris asked.

Troop Leader Buttonwood shrugged. "It's up to you to decide."

"It's a story," Julianna said. "My dad likes to tell stories about the **old Cropsey ghost** when we go on camping trips. Telling scary stories is part of camping."

"Could be," Troop Leader Buttonwood said. "But as your Beaver Scout troop leader, it's my job to **warn you just the same**. Since he's part bear, Triple F hibernates. But unlike other bears, he sleeps in the summer—right around now. And he doesn't like his sleep to be disturbed. So if you go out into the woods, be **very, very quiet**."

"Is the Ferocious Furry Frog a vegetarian?" Sage asked nervously.

"Oh no! He's a meat eater," Troop Leader Buttonwood told her.

"But he doesn't eat campers, right?" Sage asked.

"Oh, come on," Louie said. He scratched the big Band-Aid that was covering the burn on his nose. "A giant, hairy frog that eats campers? Who would believe that?"

"Me," Mike said.

"It could be possible," Max added.

It was the first time George had ever heard either of them disagree with Louie. And it was the first time George ever agreed with Louie. He thought Triple F was just a story, too.

Suddenly, George stood up. He had to go to the bathroom. He looked around the campsite. "Hey, where's the toilet?" he asked Troop Leader Buttonwood.

"Someone stole the toilet." Chris laughed. "This is a case for Toiletman!"

George frowned. "No, come on. There has to be an outhouse at least."

"I'm afraid not." Troop Leader Buttonwood shook his head. "You have to go in the woods."

George gulped. **The woods?** Where Triple F lived? Not that George believed the story was true or anything. *But still.*

"Bring your flashlight," Troop Leader Buttonwood told him. "Just don't go far. You'll be fine."

Really? George wasn't so sure. Who knew what could be waiting for him once he got into **the woods alone**?

Chapter 8

"It's not so dark, it's not so dark," George chanted to himself as he walked into the woods. **But it *was* dark.** Even with the full moon overhead and a flashlight.

The campsite wasn't far away. He was close enough to hear Louie playing his guitar. If George could hear the other scouts, then they could hear him if he had to scream for help. What could go wrong?

Uh-oh!

George felt something **bouncing up and down** inside his belly. Something that bing-bonged and ping-ponged.

Something even scarier than being in the woods alone. **The super burp was back!**

George had to stop that burp. He shut his lips tight and held his nose. He swallowed really hard, trying to force the burp back down his throat.

But the super burp had been kept down for too long. **It needed to break free!**

The bubbles bounced their way into George's chest. They bing-bonged up into his throat and ping-ponged all the way to his mouth. They tickled his tongue and danced around his teeth. And then . . .

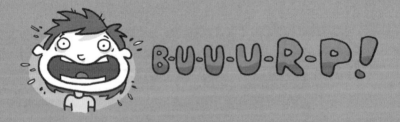

B·U·U·U·R·P!

George let out a burp so loud it woke the animals! *Squeak! Chirp! Chatter!* The animals began answering George's call of the wild.

The next thing George knew, **he was going wild**. *"Ribbit! Ribbit! ROAR!"* his mouth shouted out. Then he started hopping like a frog.

"Ribbit! Ribbit! ROAR!" George's mouth shouted again.

"AAAHHHHHH!!!!"

George's ears heard **shouts and screaming** coming from the campsite.

"Aaaahhh!" George heard Louie shout. "It's that Triple F monster! He's real!"

"Oh no! My Georgie is trapped in the woods with a monster!" Sage cried out.

George wanted to shout that he wasn't Sage's Georgie and he wasn't Triple F. But all that came out was, *"Ribbit! Ribbit! ROAR!"*

George's legs scrambled over to a nearby tree. His back started scratching against the tree bark like a big bear. *"Ribbit! Ribbit! ROAR!"* his mouth shouted.

A moment later, all the scouts and Troop Leader Buttonwood surrounded him. **A flashlight was pointed right at his eyes.** Julianna was holding it.

"George! All that noise! It was you!" Julianna shouted. Everybody looked really, really mad. All except Alex. He knew what was going on.

Then George felt something go pop! It was like **a bee stinger bursting a balloon** in the bottom of his belly. The air rushed right out of him. The super burp was gone.

"George!" the troop leader shouted. "Why were you making all those noises? You scared the whole troop!"

George opened his mouth to say, "I'm sorry." And that's exactly what came out.

"Don't try anything like that again," Troop Leader Buttonwood told him. "There's no badge for practical joking, you know."

"Yes, sir," George answered.

"I knew it was him all the time," Louie said as he picked **a piece of white marshmallow booger** out of his nostril. "He didn't scare me one bit."

"Now come on," Troop Leader Buttonwood said. He turned and tripped over a rock. "I'm okay," he told the kids. "I *meant* to do that. To show you there was a rock there. Don't trip over it when you walk back to the campsite."

"Um . . . I can't go back yet," George told him.

"Why not?" Troop Leader Buttonwood asked.

"Because I still have to . . . well . . . **you know**," George answered.

"Oh." The troop leader understood. "Okay. But hurry up. It's almost time for lights out. And no more fooling around."

George nodded and waited for everyone to leave. **Toilet or no toilet**, he had to *go* now. There were some things even the super burp couldn't control.

Chapter 9

"You're supposed to wave the flyswatter at the fly," Louie told Max and Mike early the next morning as Troop 307 went on their nature hike in the woods. "When you guys volunteered to swat all the flies that came near me, I thought you would do it right."

"Sorry, Louie," Max said.

"We'll swat the next fly," Mike added. "You'll see."

Suddenly, a fly landed right on Louie's nose. Max and Mike **slammed their swatters** right down on it.

"Ouch!"

Louie shouted. "What did you do that for?"

"We were swatting the fly," Max explained.

"But we missed," Mike added.

Louie scowled and rubbed the bandage that was covering his **burned, sore nose**. "This hike is the pits," he said.

Actually, Louie wasn't the only kid who felt that way. Beaver Scout Troop 307 had been hiking in the woods for hours. Or at least it seemed that way to George. But they didn't seem to be getting anywhere. They were just going around and around in circles.

"I think we walked past that **same tree** a little while ago," Alex told Troop Leader Buttonwood.

"How do you know if it's the same tree?" Louie asked Alex. "All these trees look alike."

"Look." Alex pointed to a **small brown nest** high up in the branches. "I already spotted that yellow-bellied sapsucker in her nest twenty minutes ago.

I checked it off on my list. I'm really close to getting that bird-watching badge."

"That's **a dweeby badge**," Louie told Alex.

"It is not," Alex insisted. "There are no dweeby Beaver Scout badges."

"Boys, stop arguing," Troop Leader Buttonwood said. "I'm trying to figure out where we are."

"You mean you don't really know?" Sage asked him.

"Well, we traveled off the trail," Troop Leader Buttonwood said. "But don't worry. I have a map of the Beaver Scout campgrounds." He reached into his backpack and dug around. "**At least I thought I brought the map.** Unless . . ."

"*Unless?*" Julianna asked him.

"Unless I didn't. I was studying it this morning to see which trail to take, and **I must have left it in my tent**."

Sage looked like she was going to cry. "Oh no. We're lost in the woods!"

Just then a brown-and-black chipmunk raced across the path. Louie jumped and **let out a scream**.

George laughed. "It's just a chipmunk, Louie," he said. "Sheesh."

"That wasn't a chipmunk. It was a big rat," Louie said. He looked at Max and Mike. "Wasn't it, you guys?"

"Well, it had a tail," Max said. "Rats have tails."

"And it was sorta fat," Mike added. "Rats are fat . . . sometimes."

"See?" Louie told George. "Ouch! I think I just got stung by something."

"I hate bugs!" Louie shouted. "And I

hate rats. What kind of woods are these, anyway?"

Sage grabbed George's arm. "I'm glad you're here to protect me from the **wild rats and mosquitoes**."

George yanked away his arm. Who was going to protect *him* from Sage?

"I know we're supposed to be heading north," Troop Leader Buttonwood said. "But which way is north?" He looked around. "The sun rises in the east and sets in the west. Does anyone remember where the sunrise started?"

"My feet are sweating in these boots," Sage complained. **"They're going to stink."**

"That's because your boots are made of rubber," Alex told her. "Rubber makes your feet sweaty."

"Now you tell me." Sage looked at Julianna. "My stinky, sweaty feet are all your fault."

"It's not my fault," Julianna insisted.

"Kids, calm down," Troop Leader Buttonwood insisted. "I can figure this out, I think."

"You *think*?" Sage shouted.

"I'll get us out of this." Louie reached into his backpack and pulled out a cell phone. "I'll call my dad. He'll send **a park ranger** or someone to help us." He looked down at the phone. "Hey! I'm not getting any service. What kind of uncivilized woods are these, anyway?"

"Woods are *supposed* to be uncivilized," George said. "That's the **whole point**."

"Yeah, well, I want to get back to civilization," Louie said. "And how am I supposed to do that without a cell phone?"

"With this," Julianna said. She **held up the compass** around her neck. "The arrow will tell us which way is north."

"Great!" Troop Leader Buttonwood said.

"You saved us!" Sage exclaimed.

George looked over at Louie as the troop hiked north. "And you didn't want Julianna to come on this camping trip."

Louie rolled his eyes. "So she has a necklace with an arrow. **Big deal.**"

"Not a necklace, a compass," Julianna corrected him.

"And it's a *huge* deal," Alex said. "It'll help us get back to the campsite."

"It's also earning Julianna her **Explorer badge**," Troop Leader Buttonwood said.

"Cool beans!" Chris exclaimed.

"Congratulations. And I'm sorry for getting mad before," Sage told Julianna.

"Hey, Louie?" George asked. "Isn't the Explorer badge the only one your brother Sam *didn't* get?"

Louie didn't say a word. He just looked ahead and kept hiking.

George grinned. That compass really *was* something special. It was the only thing George had ever seen that could shut Louie up.

Chapter 10

By the time Troop 307 got back to the campsite, they were hot, tired, and **really, really hungry**.

"We're going to have hamburgers," Troop Leader Buttonwood told the troops. "But I think we're running a little low on firewood."

"I'll go get some," George said. He wanted to be extra helpful to make up for **his burp-out last night**.

"Great," Troop Leader Buttonwood said. "We don't need a lot because we're going to put the fire

out right after lunch. So just get some twigs and a few thick branches."

"I'll help you, Georgie," Sage said.

"I can handle it," George told her. Then he hurried into the woods.

It was amazing how *not* scary the woods were in the daylight. Last night it had been really creepy out there. But now George thought it was **kind of nice to be alone**.

Crack.

But *was* he alone?

Crack.

George heard a noise again. It sounded like a twig breaking under someone's foot. Oh no! Was Sage following him again?

George turned. But he didn't see Sage.

Crack.

There it was again.

"Ribbit . . ."

Okay. That wasn't Sage.

"ROAR!"

Gulp. Now George knew for sure he *wasn't* alone.

Two big green paws attached to two big, green, and furry arms spread apart the bushes.

Holy guacamole!

Suddenly George found himself standing face-to-face with . . . **Triple F**.

This—this *thing*—was real, and it was **at least eight feet tall**.

"Rrroar! Ribbit! Rrroar!" The Ferocious Furry Frog growled at George. Then it hopped toward him.

George gulped. He blinked his eyes. He still couldn't believe what he was seeing!

Triple F was really *real*! And from the way it was smacking its **big, green lips**, it was clearly hungry! Unfortunately, the only thing on the menu was George.

This was about as *ba-a-ad* as things could get. **And then things got worse!**

Oh no! A super burp

was bing-bonging around in George's belly.

"*Ribbit! Roar!*" Triple F growled.

Bing-bong! Ping-pong!

"*Ribbit . . .*"

Bing-bong . . .

"*Ribbit . . .*"

George let out **a huge, superloud super burp**. The force of the burp shook the trees so hard, leaves fell off.

Triple F's frog eyes bugged out at the sound. The monster blinked as if it couldn't believe what it was seeing. The fur stood up on its back.

Triple F let out a mighty "*Ribbit! Roar!*" He stared at George. And then . . .

it hopped off into the forest as fast as its frog legs could go. George couldn't believe it. **The super burp had scared off Triple F!**

And then, suddenly, George felt something pop in his belly. All the air rushed out of him. The super burp was gone. But George was still there. And he knew exactly what he had to do!

Run!

"What do you mean, *Where's the wood?*" George asked his friends a

few minutes later when he got to the campsite. "Didn't you hear what I just told you? **I saw Triple F.** And I scared it away."

"All I hear is my stomach grumbling," Louie told him. "And we can't cook the hamburgers until we have some wood."

"But it was huge," George said. "It could have eaten us all. Those humongous animal tracks we saw when

we got here yesterday? I bet those were Triple F's! And you should have heard it roar."

"We heard something that sounded like a loud frog *ribbit*," Julianna said. "Only it was you . . . again."

"Just like last night," Sage said.

George looked at Alex. Not even his best friend believed him. Of course it was

hard to believe . . . **a gigantic, furry frog scared off by a super burp**—unless you were there to see it.

This really stunk. George deserved a merit badge for bravery. For once the super burp had done something right. **And nobody cared.**

Chapter 11

"And here's your Explorer badge," Troop Leader Buttonwood said at the next troop meeting. He handed Julianna a badge **with a telescope on it**.

Julianna was beaming. "Thanks," she said.

Everyone in the troop was taking home badges to sew onto their uniforms.

"Did you see **my Bird-Watching badge**?" Alex asked George. "It's got a robin on it."

"Georgie, look!" Sage shoved a badge with a flower on it under George's nose. "I got it for identifying wildflowers. Isn't it adorable?"

George rolled his eyes. You didn't call Beaver Scout badges **adorable**.

"Your Water Safety badge is great," Sage went on. "Every time I see you wearing it, I'll remember how you **saved my life**."

George turned to Chris. "Let me see your Art badge again."

"Sure!" Chris said. Chris had made a huge Toiletman statue out of papier-mâché. He had brought it to the meeting to show everyone. A **roll of toilet paper** hung from Toiletman's plunger.

George laughed. "Nice job, dude," he said. "Now we're all set for the next camping trip!"

Chris smiled. "Exactly. A Beaver Scout is always prepared," he joked.

Forget toilet paper, George was prepared in case something even worse came up on the next camping trip. **Triple F repellant.** And it came in the form of the magical super burp. Hey, at least it was good for something.

About the Author

Nancy Krulik is the author of more than 150 books for children and young adults including three *New York Times* best sellers and the popular Katie Kazoo, Switcheroo books. She lives in New York City with her family, and many of George Brown's escapades are based on things her own kids have done. (No one delivers a good burp quite like Nancy's son, Ian!) Nancy's favorite thing to do is laugh, which comes in pretty handy when you're trying to write funny books!

About the Illustrator

Aaron Blecha was raised by a school of giant squid in Wisconsin and now lives with his family by the English seaside. He works as an artist designing toys, animating cartoons, and illustrating books, including the Zombiekins and The Rotten Adventures of Zachary Ruthless series. You can enjoy more of his weird creations at www.monstersquid.com.